The Big Storm

by Robin Reid

illustrated by Kirk-Albert Etienne

SCHOLASTIC INC.

New York   Toronto   London   Auckland   Sydney
Mexico City   New Delhi   Hong Kong   Buenos Aires

Based on the TV series *Little Bill*® created by Bill Cosby as seen on Nick Jr.®

ISBN 0-439-40579-3

12 11 10 9 8 7 6 5 4 3 2 1   2 3 4 5 6 7/0

Printed in the U.S.A.

First Scholastic printing, September 2002

Rain was pounding against the window as Little Bill got ready for bed. "Can you read *Teddy and the Tugboats* to me, Mama?" Little Bill asked. "We can help Teddy save the tugboats from the big storm. Toot! Toot!"

"Toot! Toot!" said Brenda. "First let's get *you* safely into bed."

As Little Bill got under the covers, lightning flashed outside his window and then . . . *kaboom!* There was a loud crash of thunder.

KABOOM!

Little Bill grabbed Brenda's arm. "I don't like lightning and thunder, Mama," he said. "They're so scary and loud."

"I know, baby," said Brenda. "That's why I'm here. And we'd better hurry—the tugboats need our help."

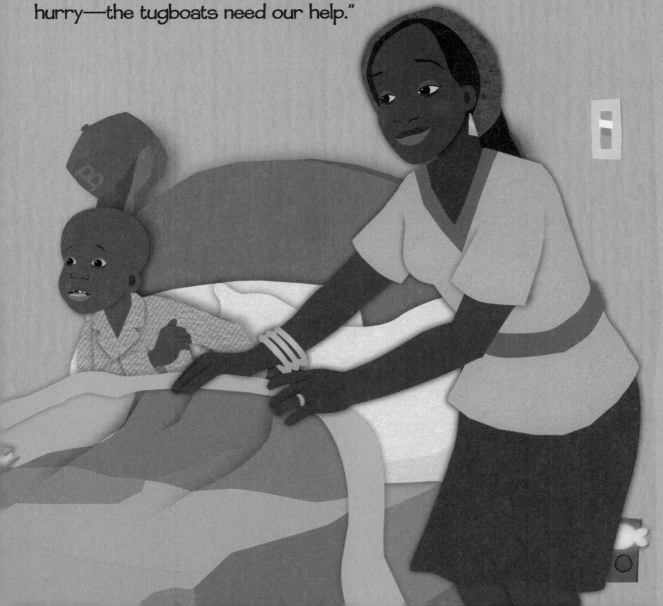

Suddenly all the lights in the room went out—even the guppy night-light!

"What happened, Mama?" asked Little Bill.

"I think the storm made the lights go out," she answered.

Little Bill moved closer to Brenda. "Can you turn them back on?"

"I can't, Little Bill, but I'm sure they'll come back on in no time," said Brenda. She pointed out the window. "Look, the lights in all the houses on our street have gone out too."

Just then Little Bill spotted some brightly colored lights in the doorway.

"Little Bill, I brought you some glow sticks," April said as she waved her arms. "They're fun to play with in the dark."

"Cool!" said Little Bill. "We can use them as a laser light shield."

April laughed. "Yeah, they can protect us as we find our way back to our spaceship!"

Outside, lightning struck again and thunder rumbled. *Kaboom!* Little Bill jumped at the loud sound.

"Don't worry, Little Bill," April said. "Whenever I hear thunder, I imagine that the clouds are playing basketball. If they make a basket, the thunder goes wild—*kaboom!*"

"Kaboom! Kaboom! Two points for the clouds!" shouted Little Bill.

A moment later Little Bill saw a small flickering light in the doorway. "Hey, Little Bill," called Bobby. "I made you something. I call it 'Bobby's special stormy night-light.'"

"It looks like a candle in a big jar to me," said April.

"Exactly!" said Bobby. "I made it for my *favorite* little brother."

Little Bill laughed. "I'm your *only* little brother!"

"I can't wait for more thunder," Bobby said.
"Not me," said Little Bill. "It's too loud."

"Of course it's loud," said Bobby. "The lightning is moving through the sky at supersonic speed—"

"Faster than a rocket ship?" asked Little Bill.

Bobby nodded. "Oh, yeah! So fast that it makes a big noise—*kaboom!*"

Soon Alice the Great came into the room. "I brought this old oil lamp to help you and Mama read," she said.

"I like that lamp!" Little Bill exclaimed. "How does it work?"

"By burning oil. When I was your age, we used these lamps—so we didn't worry about losing our lights during a storm!"

The thunder rumbled again.

"Did you worry about thunder and lightning when you were my age?" Little Bill asked Alice the Great.

"I sure did," said Alice the Great. "But now whenever I hear thunder, I imagine that Mother Nature is happy, so she's clapping. *Kaboom!*"

"Mother Nature must be clapping her hands *and* stomping her feet!" said Little Bill.

"Here you all are," said Big Bill. "I brought a flashlight. But it looks like you have plenty of light."

Outside the thunder exploded.

Big Bill jumped. "I don't like thunder," he said. "It's so loud."

"Don't worry," said Little Bill. "Mother Nature's just so happy watching a basketball game that she's clapping her hands and stomping her feet!"

Big Bill laughed. "It must be a really exciting game!"

At that moment there was a flicker and all the lights came back on.
"We've got lights, we've got lights!" sang Little Bill.

"Well," said Big Bill, "now that the lights are back on, let's turn them off and go to sleep."

"But we can't go to sleep yet," said Little Bill, "Teddy and the tugboats still need our help."

Teddy and the Tugboats

And everyone stayed up to help Teddy save the tugboats from the big storm.

TOOT!
TOOT!

Teddy and the Tugboats